DISTANT LIGHTS

DISTANT LIGHTS

AND OTHER ADVENTURE STORIES
Compiled by the Editors
of
Highlights for Children

Compilation copyright © 1994 by Highlights for Children
Contents copyright by Highlights for Children
Published by Highlights for Children, Inc.
P.O. Box 18201
Columbus, Ohio 43218-0201
Printed in the United States of America

ISBN 0-87534-622-7

Highlights Highlights is a registered trademark of Highlights for Children, Inc.

CONTENTS

DISTANT LIGHTS

By F. Anthony Reckart

Mike Brandon shivered as he watched his cousin Pierre bait one of his traps. Pierre's fingers moved expertly, despite the bitter cold. He grinned at Mike standing by the dog sled. "Just one more trap," he said, "then we'll head back to the cabin. It's going to get very cold when night comes." Mike couldn't see how it could possibly get any colder. The thermometer back at the trading post they had left an hour ago read thirty below zero.

"I guess you've never seen such cold before, eh, Mike?" asked Pierre as he came back to start the dogs. His team of Huskies was one of the finest for miles around. The dogs were barking and snapping in the razor-sharp air and were glad to start moving. As Mike stood on the back of the sled, his cousin jogged alongside shouting, "Mush, mush!" to the scrambling dogs.

In his home state of Illinois, Mike had never seen anything like the Canadian wilds. The Yukon was a vast lonely country where one depended on strength and skill to survive. As the sled moved over the blanket of white, the Northern lights shimmered like a huge forest fire along a horizon of barren, wind-swept slopes. Mike was glad he had come for a visit.

After traveling about half an hour, Pierre stopped the dogs and unloaded the last of the steel traps from the sled. "You stay here, Mike," he said. "I'm going over on the other side of that slope to set this trap. I won't be long."

The cold bit its way through Mike's heavy furs and stung his face. Minutes dragged by, and he began to wonder what was keeping Pierre. He felt an urge to call out as night settled its mantle of darkness over the forest. Then he heard a muffled cry coming from the direction Pierre had gone.

Mike walked to the top of the rise and looked around. He couldn't see very far because of the dark and the deceiving shadows. The lead dog growled as if to say something was wrong. Mike cupped his hands to his mouth and called out. The forest seemed to smother the sound of his voice before it got inches away from his lips.

After an agonizing silence Mike heard a weak cry close to where he stood. It was Pierre lying on his side in the snow near a thick underbrush. One look at his cousin's pain-twisted face told him something terrible had happened.

"Mike," gasped Pierre through gritted teeth, "I think I have broken my hip. I stepped in a hole and twisted my leg. I can barely move it." Pierre tried to pull himself upright, but the effort was too great and he lost consciousness.

The realization that he was alone, deep in the Canadian wilds, shocked Mike so he couldn't move. The barking Huskies roused him at last. He knew he had to do something and do it quickly. Better to die trying to live than to give up without a struggle. He would have to get Pierre back to the trading post as fast as possible.

As in a nightmare, Mike pulled and tugged Pierre as gently as he could back to the sled. Getting Pierre onto the sled and wrapping him in blankets kept his mind from thinking about the hopelessness of getting back to the trading post in the darkness. At last he started the dogs back along the trail.

The Huskies knew something was wrong and dug in for all they were worth. With each mile Mike's heart rose until, after several hours, he saw that the dogs had left the trail. Somewhere in the gloom they had lost it. For all Mike knew, they were heading for the Arctic Ocean.

This bitter discouragement was replaced by a warm and sleepy desire to sit down and rest. Mike was about to stop the dogs when he realized he was experiencing one of the symptoms of freezing to death. The ruthless North was reaching for his throat and he was too weary to fight back. He caught a glimpse of two wolves watching silently from between some trees off to one side.

Mike tried to keep awake by shouting at the dogs until at last he began to stagger. Suddenly the lead dog started barking furiously. As in a dream Mike lifted his head, and through half-shut eyes he saw distant lights. They came from the glow of a fire showing through square windows. Fire meant warmth, food, and help for Pierre. The lead dog's excited barking was taken up by some of the others, and dark forms came hurrying from the trading post. Mike knew they were safe at last. The dogs had led him to the trading post.

The Diver

By Isabelle Ziegler

When the two boys reached the top of the hill, Danny stopped and wiped the sweat from his face. Then he picked up a stone, wound up like a pitcher, and threw it at a clump of cactus.

"I don't see why you want to come up here EVERY afternoon," he said to his friend Esteban. "Boy, I'd like to see a good baseball game for a change." He sat down on a large rock and looked up at the cliff. Esteban stood beside him, too excited to sit down.

"Baseball, baseball," the Mexican boy said. "A man hits a little ball with a club, then chases it. Then nobody does anything."

"How many times do I have to explain," Danny said. "The batter doesn't chase the ball. Someone else chases the ball."

But Esteban wasn't listening. "If we didn't come every day, we might miss El Gato," he said. "He doesn't dive off the cliff every day—just when he needs the money."

"I don't see anything so big about diving from a cliff. He can swim, can't he?"

"You don't know what you are talking about," Esteban responded. "El Gato dives into a narrow slit of water between terrible rocks. That is the most dangerous thing in the world except fighting the bulls."

Esteban jumped up. "Look! It's El Gato! He's going to dive today. Come on, let's go up to the next hill so we can see him hit the water."

The cliff divers at Acapulco give their performance just at sunset, and the sun was about to fall behind the Pacific Ocean when the boys reached the top of the second hill. Even Danny held his breath as he watched the young man dive almost straight down into the narrow body of water between the rocky cliffs.

But when the performance was over and the boys were running down the hill, Danny said he still didn't think it was all that big. He guessed he could do it himself.

Esteban looked shocked. "What a big boast you make! You would be dead in half a minute."

Before he left his friend to go back to the hotel, Danny said, "I won the diving medal at camp last summer. Best diver among the twelve-year-olds. I was really a better diver than the older boys, too."

"That's baby stuff," Esteban said. "Cliff diving is very difficult."

"Well, you can come and watch me," Danny said. "Tomorrow morning."

"You wouldn't dare."

"Come and see."

The next morning Danny put on his swimming trunks and told his parents he wasn't going to the beach—he and Esteban had something else to do.

He hurried away before they could ask him any questions and climbed the first hill, all the time looking back for Esteban. He hoped Esteban believed him because it wouldn't be any fun without someone to watch him. Esteban still hadn't appeared when he reached the hill that led to the top of the cliff. He looked up. It was steeper and rockier than it had looked from the other hill, but he could climb it all right.

A third of the way up, he stopped to get his breath. It was all rock now, and his feet kept slipping. Big blisters were popping out on his hands.

Across the hill below he thought he saw Esteban's red shirt. He wanted to wave, but he needed both hands to hang onto the rocks. Then all of a sudden he was nowhere. He was hanging onto a rock with his hands, but his feet were dangling over the water. With a violent swing he pulled himself up to a ledge and clung to the wall of rock. He looked up. The next ledge seemed about the height of two men. He looked down—rocks and an almost invisible slit of water. The ledge itself was long, but no wider than the length of his feet. In spite of the heat he felt frozen to the rock. He couldn't go up. . . . If he dived . . . but he couldn't. He would have to stand here all day until the divers came up in the late afternoon. And he knew he couldn't do that.

He felt that a whole day must have passed—actually it was less than ten minutes—when he heard voices echo against the rock. Then they stopped, and he almost cried. A minute later he heard a man's voice shouting, "Do not move. Do not move. I will help you. El Gato comes."

Then the voice was coming from the ledge directly above him. "You will attach the rope to yourself. Attach it firmly. I will pull you up to where I stand."

Danny had another bad moment when he had to take his bleeding hands from the rocky wall. Then he was safe on the wide ledge with El Gato.

14

The man's voice was serious but kind. "It is not yet over," he said. "Do you want me to take you down, or do we dive? Esteban, who is waiting on the hill, tells me you swim well and dive well."

Danny looked down into the water. With El Gato beside him, he thought, it didn't seem so small or so far away "I was the best . . . no, I was the second-best diver at the camp—I think that I can swim better than I dive, but I'll try this."

"This is the halfway point," El Gato said. "It is not difficult. I did it with ease when I was your age. But it is for you to say."

Should he dive, or should he let El Gato carry him down like a sack of cement? He took a deep breath. "Show me how to do it," he said finally.

El Gato told Danny how he must stand, how many steps to take, how he must dive. "You will see that it is no more difficult than diving from the edge of a swimming pool."

He smiled, Danny tried to smile, and then they dived, El Gato waiting until Danny's feet had left the cliff. They surfaced together.

A few minutes later Esteban came running across the sandbar where Danny was still spitting out the salt water he had swallowed.

"How brave you were and how well you dived," Esteban said. "Were you not afraid?"

Danny looked at El Gato, who merely smiled. "Afraid of what? No . . . " Then he grinned. "To tell you the truth, I was scared stiff . . . me and my big mouth. If it hadn't been for El Gato . . . how did he happen to be there anyhow?"

"I came to the beach," Esteban explained. "I am afraid I did not believe you yesterday when you said you would try to dive. When your father told me you had already left, I knew what you had decided to do. I ran for El Gato."

"I must leave you now," El Gato said, "for a long siesta before the big leap."

"We'll be watching you," Danny said. "I'll bring my father. He doesn't know that diving is the most exciting and most dangerous thing in the world."

"More exciting than baseball?" Esteban asked.

Tiger on Jefferson Boulevard

By Roger J. Crain

Patty could hardly wait. She had gotten her things together early because she didn't want to be late, tonight of all nights. All her teammates and their parents would be at the church hall at seven o'clock for the basketball awards ceremony.

"It's ten to seven, Dad," said Patty. She was getting warm standing by the door in her coat.

"OK, Patty, I'll be right with you," her dad said. He took a last sip of tea and pushed away from the dinner table.

"This is going to be fun," said Patty as she opened the front door. The street was quiet, and overhead several dozen stars winked at her from the bitterly cold night sky. The moon was almost too bright to look at, but it cast only a chill light on the snow.

Patty listened to the dry snow crunching under her feet. She heard a car start up several blocks away, and then she heard a dull humming noise from an airplane high up in the sky. The noise of the jet's engines seemed to come from way behind the moving dot of light that was the plane itself. But as the noise of the plane faded away, Patty heard a new noise, much closer. She heard a scratching noise from under the family car. She bent down and then knelt in the snow to see under the car.

"Did you lose something?" asked her dad.

Patty jumped in surprise and shook her head. "No, Dad, but I think I heard something moving under the car."

"It's probably just the wind."

"No, it was a scratching noise." Patty looked again, and then she saw it. It was a fluffy tan ball with two yellow eyes. "It's Tiger," she cried out in surprise. "Dad, it's Tiger, Mrs. Anderson's cat!"

Patty's dad knelt in the snow and peered beneath the car. "It *is* Tiger!" he exclaimed. "Here, Tiger, come here, kitty."

Tiger meowed quietly and crawled out from beneath the car. Patty picked up the kitten and stroked its fur. Tiger shivered, and there was a coating of frost on the kitten's whiskers. Suddenly the kitten shook violently with the cold. "Dad," said Patty, "he's almost frozen."

"He must have gotten out by accident. Mrs. Anderson doesn't ever let Tiger run loose."

Patty held the frightened kitten close to her coat. "I'll bring him into the house," she said as she started to walk back to the porch.

"That wouldn't be a good idea, Patty. Your brother is very allergic to cats."

Patty stopped and held the cat close. "Should I return him to Mrs. Anderson?" she asked.

Her father looked at Patty closely. "You'll be late for the awards."

Patty thought about this problem for a moment, and then made up her mind. "I'm going to return Tiger to Mrs. Anderson, Dad. I can't leave him out here to freeze."

"I thought that's what you would do."

"I'll be back as soon as I can," said Patty as she started off down the street. Mrs. Anderson's house was near the end of the block, and Patty had to walk slowly because she didn't want to slip and fall on top of Tiger.

As Patty climbed the front porch stairs she noticed that Mrs. Anderson's house was dark inside.

She rang the doorbell and waited. No one answered. She tried again a few moments later, but still no one answered. Mrs. Anderson hardly ever went outside when it was this cold, so Patty guessed that the elderly lady was probably asleep. Patty didn't know what to do.

She tried ringing the doorbell once more. When there was no answer Patty decided to ask another neighbor to take care of Tiger for the night. Patty started down the porch stairs and then stopped. She heard something inside the house, something that fell with a crash.

As she went around the side of the house to investigate, Tiger began squirming suddenly, scratching and fighting against Patty's grip. Something was making the kitten terribly frightened, and Tiger clawed and wrestled so desperately that Patty was forced to put him down on the porch. As soon as Patty released him, Tiger streaked out to the sidewalk. But as Patty was straightening up, she discovered the reason for the kitten's fear. She smelled smoke!

The girl stood up quickly and, on tiptoe, looked through the window into Mrs. Anderson's house. There were flames inside and they were spreading quickly. The house was on fire!

Patty turned around and yelled for her dad. But he was inside the car and couldn't hear her call over the noise of the car's engine. Patty started to run toward her father's car. Then she suddenly remembered that Mrs. Anderson was probably asleep upstairs. And the older woman couldn't hear the doorbell!

Patty was frightened. She jumped back instinctively when an angry yellow flare of fire shot up past the window.

She remembered that Mrs. Anderson slept in a room directly over the living room downstairs. The leaping flames were right beneath her. Patty had to warn her to get out of the house.

As Patty looked around for something with which she could warn Mrs. Anderson, she spotted Tiger on the sidewalk. She remembered playing with Tiger in the rock garden last summer. Patty began digging frantically. Snow and dirt flew in all directions until she found what she was looking for. She kicked sharply, and the large flat rock broke free from the ice.

Patty picked up the rock and ran out onto the lawn. She took careful aim and then threw the rock straight through Mrs. Anderson's bedroom window. The glass broke with a terribly loud crash, and part of the wooden frame clattered down to the ground. But the sudden noise and blast of cold air did the trick.

Seconds later Mrs. Anderson appeared at her shattered window. "Fire! Mrs. Anderson, your house is on fire!" Patty yelled.

Mrs. Anderson looked confused; she hadn't heard. Patty shouted, "Fire!" as loud as she could, and she pointed to the flames. The elderly woman disappeared from the window. A few seconds later Mrs. Anderson threw open the front door, and she weakly walked out, followed by a huge blast of smoke and hot air.

Patty's dad saw the smoke and ran to call the fire department. Patty helped Mrs. Anderson to their house, and Tiger followed them inside. They heard sirens a few minutes later as the fire engines roared to a stop in the icy street. Firemen shouted, red lights flashed angrily, and soon many neighbors were outside watching the firemen save Mrs. Anderson's house.

But Patty didn't want to watch the firemen. She and her mom and dad and Mrs. Anderson were sitting around their kitchen table drinking cups of hot chocolate.

"Your daughter saved my life," said Mrs. Anderson. "I don't know how to thank you."

Patty smiled from ear to ear and stroked Tiger, who was asleep in a box at her feet. At this moment, she didn't care at all about missing the basketball awards.

Friendly Cactus

By Jim Martin

Suddenly Ronnie was afraid. It seemed a long time since he had left the other boys and Mr. Adams—maybe an hour. Around him, no matter which way he turned, everything in the desert looked strange. He stubbed his foot against a sharp black rock and almost fell into the prickly arms of a cholla cactus. He quickly backed away from it, more alarmed than ever.

Above him the sun rolled across the sky like a great ball of fire. Far off in the distance, bare gray mountains shimmered in the heat. The dry, hot desert stretched for miles in every direction. It was covered with rock piles, sand, dry bushes, and what looked to him like a million kinds of cacti. And he knew he was lost!

Mr. Adams, who lived near Ronnie's home, had agreed to take some of the neighborhood boys, along with his own sons, on an outing into the desert. Ronnie had only recently come with his parents to live in Arizona. Because he had never been in the desert, he was glad when Mr. Adams invited him to go.

As they rode along, Mr. Adams pointed out and named a lot of cacti. Some had funny names. The very tall ones scattered over the desert like thorny telephone poles, their huge arms reaching upward, were saguaro. Some that looked like bunches of long whips were ocotillo. Others with large flat thorny leaves were prickly pear. There were also hedgehog, barrel, and peanut cactus.

They had parked the station wagon near a tall saguaro and started out on a hike through the trackless desert. They had gone some distance when Ronnie, behind the others, decided it would be fun to dodge from sight behind some rocks and take a shortcut back to the station wagon.

He imagined the astonishment on the faces of the other boys when they came back by a longer trail and found him there ahead of them.

Now Ronnie wished he hadn't done it, because somehow everything was all turned around and he didn't know which way to go.

He darted around jagged rock piles, between cacti, and through dry sandy washes where desert willow and palo verde trees grew. The other boys were nowhere in sight. And now he was so thirsty he could hardly swallow.

He walked in one direction, then turned and went the other way. Sweat dried on his face as soon as it started. His tongue was so dry he couldn't even lick his lips. He lost all track of time, but he knew he had been wandering around for quite a while.

He looked at the sun. It was traveling fast toward the ridge of mountains that hemmed in the desert on one side.

That way must be west. But was that the right direction to go to reach the station wagon? What would happen to him if he couldn't find the way back to it and night came? All alone in the desert at night, where even the cacti were unfriendly, ready to stick him with their sharp thorns if he went near them! The thought filled him with terror. It wouldn't be so bad if only another boy were with him.

Blindly he started to run. Fear drove him on and on. He had to get out of the desert before night. He had to—

Suddenly he stopped and remembered. He was doing just what those two boys did last summer. The story had been in the newspapers. They had been lost too, and they had run and run and had not been found.

Startled, he stood still and listened. It seemed as if he heard his father saying what he had often said. "Remember there's always a way out of every difficulty, Ronnie. Learn to think for yourself, and you will find a solution."

Tense and hot, he stared down at the scorching sand at his feet. Surely Mr. Adams would be looking for him. If he stood still they were certain to find him sometime. But if they didn't come soon, where could he get a drink of water? He felt as if he were burning up inside, and he had never been so thirsty in his whole life.

He squinted off into the hazy distance. Cacti were growing all around him. They were alive. A barrel cactus! That was the answer. Mr. Adams had said that the water stored in the barrel cactus had often saved people's lives.

Ronnie straightened his shoulders and walked slowly until he saw a cactus shaped like a barrel. He reached for the Scout hatchet hanging from his belt. Trembling with haste, he slashed at the cactus until it split open.

Water oozed out of it. Eagerly he tore out a handful of its spongy pulp and squeezed the water into his mouth. It tasted strange, but it was wet and satisfying. Soon he had all he needed. He was no longer thirsty.

Now the cacti didn't seem so unfriendly, and thoughts of spending a night alone in the desert were not so terrifying.

The sun had sunk behind the mountains when he saw Mr. Adams and the boys searching for him. He shouted and waved his arms, and they hurried to him.

"You were wise not to run," Mr. Adams said. "I was afraid you might do what those two boys did last summer. I was mighty scared."

"I was scared too," Ronnie said. "I wouldn't have been lost if I'd stopped to think sooner, because then I wouldn't have even started walking off by myself."

The Last of the Light

By Douglas Ayers

Rense pedaled as fast as he could along the dike. The canal beside him was frozen over and covered with snow, except in a few spots at the edge where families of ducks searched for food. Far down the straight, flat path of the dike Rense could see his home and the cozy puffs of smoke streaming from its chimney.

"Good," he thought. "I'm glad she felt well enough to keep the fire going. The house will be nice and warm." Rense's bright striped scarf sailed behind him as he put on speed to cover the last stretch of road. He leaned his bicycle against the house at one side of the back door and gathered his stack of books from his backpack. At the other side of the doorway leaned another bicycle. That meant the nurse was still here.

Rense closed the door quietly behind him and dropped his books on a chair. The little kitchen was warm. A fire burned in the stove where the kettle was just beginning to boil. A tray was set out on the blue-painted table, with patterned mugs and a plate of apple cake. The cake was still warm and smelled spicy and good.

"Mama, I'm home," Rense called.

Nurse Bakker appeared in the doorway of his mother's bedroom. "Just a few minutes, Rense. I'm going to give your mother her medication. Then you can bring in the tea tray and have your after-noon snack with her."

"Sure," answered Rense. "I'll get the tea ready."

It was steaming in the pot, and Rense had just spread out his math papers and his textbook when the nurse came out of the bedroom and closed the door gently behind her. She sat down at the table beside Rense.

"Try a piece of the cake," she said. "The pastor's wife brought it for you and your mama."

Rense picked up one of the spicy squares and took a big bite. He smiled. "That's good!"

Nurse Bakker smoothed out the doily on the tea tray and nervously rearranged the mugs. "Rense," she said, "your mother's condition is a lot worse. When I got here today, she hadn't even been able to get out of bed. The fire was out, and the house was cold. She can't be left alone any longer. You have to convince her that it's time for your aunt to come live with you now. She doesn't want to admit that you and she can't manage any longer. You'll have to persuade her."

Rense didn't want to think about the illness. He knew how bad it was, and he knew that it would get even worse. But he just didn't want to think about it! What good was thinking about something when you couldn't do anything to help? He put the rest of his piece of cake down on the pale blue tabletop. "I could stay home from school," Rense said. "I could keep the fire going and cook and do everything. We don't need Aunt Sue."

He sat stiff and defiant in his chair, waiting for Nurse Bakker to answer. But she didn't say anything. Instead she placed her hand gently on Rense's shoulder. He knew what her answer would be. He knew it in his own heart.

Over and over his mother had told him, "This illness is going to take my life, Rense. We can't do anything to stop that. But we must keep it from spoiling *your* life. You must have your education. That's what has to be important—for both of us."

31

"We'll call Aunt Sue tonight," Rense told the nurse. His voice sounded shaky, and he hoped he wouldn't start to cry. The tea mugs jangled a little against each other as he lifted the tray. "Mama will like the cake."

"Rense! Rense! Come quickly!"

Both the boy and Nurse Bakker rushed into the bedroom. Mrs. Kleckner was leaning out of her bed, staring through the window. "Rense, what can we do? Look! The children!"

An enormous sheet of ice had broken free from the canal and was moving swiftly toward the sea. Rense saw a group of children huddled together in the center of the huge ice floe.

"I was watching them," said his mother. "They were skating and having fun. When I looked again, the ice was moving. You must get help! Call someone!"

Nurse Bakker hurried out of the room. "I'm telephoning for the rescue squad," she called from the living room.

Rense felt hypnotized as he stared across the water at the stranded skaters. Suddenly he felt his mother grab his hand.

"Get blankets, Rense. Build up the fire. Maybe we can be of help to those children when the rescue squad brings them in."

The boy's mind began to race. What if the rescue squad didn't arrive in time? What if the floe drifted out too far for them to reach it? The wind was strong. It was blowing the little group farther and farther out to sea as he watched.

Without even realizing it, Rense had made a decision. He grabbed his jacket and mittens as he raced out the door. "Stay with Mama," he called to the nurse. Down the rickety wooden steps to the dock he clattered, pushing his arms into his jacket sleeves as he ran. He untied the rope that held the boat fast and positioned the oars. Then he shoved his hands into his mittens and began to row.

With more strength than he knew he had, Rense pulled at the oars. Over and over he said to himself, "This is something I *can* do." He turned his head to check the position of the ice floe.

A wide stretch of dark water still separated him from the floating sheet of ice, but he could see the children more clearly now. They were huddled low on the ice, holding on to each other. Rense was too far away to see their faces, but he recognized one of them from his red-and-white jacket and black ski cap. It was Peter Notran from his grade at school. And that tiny figure next to him must be his little sister Rosalie. Peter often had to take care of her after school. Rosalie, the same name as Mama, Rense thought. He took a firmer grip on the oars and forced himself to row harder.

An hour later every one of the stranded skaters was safe and warm in Rense's house. They all clustered around the kitchen stove, drinking cups of hot cocoa and chattering about their adventure.

But Rense was silent. He sat quietly in the corner and let Nurse Bakker put ointment on his hands. They were red from the cold and raw from the chafing of wet wool against the oars.

Rense's mind was full of thought-pictures—of the way the skaters had both laughed and cried when they saw the little boat coming to save them—of the timid way little Rosalie had crept to the edge of the ice floe to crawl at last into the boat. He could see again the brave looks on the faces of the two biggest children as they watched Rense row away from the ice floe, leaving them behind for a second trip. Everyone, including Rense, knew how scared they must have been, but the little boat couldn't carry any more than three passengers at a time.

He could see, like a movie being played in his mind, Nurse Bakker kneeling at the edge of the dock, waiting to wrap the rescued children in warm blankets and hurry them into the house. And he could feel again the biting-cold wind that stung his face and tousled his hair. Even so, Rense had been glad of the wind because it helped him to reach the floating sheet of ice quickly. And then the relief when the last two skaters were safely in the boat, when Peter took the oars that Rense's numb fingers could hardly hold on to any longer. And the heavenly warmth of soft blankets, the blissful sensation of solid land underfoot as he trudged through the snow to the back door, and the tears that had come into his eyes at the sight of the children gathered in the kitchen—all safe and out of danger at last. A happy ending.

Rense felt as though he were waking from a dream when he looked up and saw Nurse Bakker smiling at him. "You can go in to see your mother now," she said quietly.

The little bedroom was hushed and almost dark. Rense thought his mother looked tired, but she looked happy, too, and content. At the foot of the bed, little Rosalie, curled up like a tired puppy, lay fast asleep.

"Nurse Bakker had to carry her into the house," Mrs. Kleckner told her son. "She was so exhausted she fell asleep as soon as you handed her up onto the dock."

"The people from the rescue squad will take her home," Rense said. "They're outside, just waiting for the others to finish their cocoa. Then I'll make us some supper."

"If you don't fall asleep first," his mother answered. "You know, Rense, I think a boy like you is just too busy to take care of a house all alone. Let's call Aunt Sue tonight and tell her it's time for her to come live with us."

"I guess that's what we have to do," said Rense.

Tokarra's Way

By Jan Peck

A tradition from Tokarra's clan commanded: "At the age of thirteen, a boy must climb the great cliff and build a fire for all the tribe to see." These were the rites for becoming a man.

Tokarra was a girl. Her father had no sons.

Tokarra awoke early, before the sun and the meadowlark. Today she was thirteen, and though small, her spirit was as strong as a bison's.

Tokarra slipped out of the cave while her father slept. She wore sandals woven from the yucca plant and carried a net bag. Inside the bag lay the fire stick, hearth stick, and the kindling. She would need these to build the signal fire.

Tokarra stopped at the bottom of the towering limestone cliff and studied the carved footholds. The men from her clan had climbed here. Some of the footholds were shallow, washed away by storms. Grasping a sharp rock, Tokarra began to deepen the holes. She would prove herself worthy—as worthy as any boy.

Out of the darkness, from behind a prickly pear cactus, slithered a snake. Its golden eyes gleamed, and it said to Tokarra, "Why do you choose the hard way when I glide to the top so easily?"

"Because," said the girl, "I would go the way of my people."

"Many have fallen by going that way," the snake said, hissing.

Tokarra looked at the cliff. It shot straight up, its shadow covering her like a giant storm cloud. She trembled. "Show me your way, then," she said.

Tokarra followed the snake into a hidden cave behind some bushes. Inside, the air was cool and damp. The tunnel gradually sloped upward. The ground felt soft under her sandals.

"Perhaps this is a better way than the way of my people," Tokarra said to herself.

As the tunnel narrowed, she had to lower her head. Rocks stuck out and scratched her arms.

Still, the path climbed steadily and seemed easier than the cliff. But then the cave closed inward, and finally Tokarra had to crawl on her belly. When the walls of the cave squeezed around her, she gasped for air.

"Just a little farther," said the snake.

Tokarra could see the light shining from a tiny hole above. "I must go back!" she cried. "This is a good way for a snake, but not for a human."

She wormed her way back out of the tunnel. After she escaped, Tokarra squinted her eyes in the light and took deep breaths.

When she opened her eyes again, the cliff hung over her like a proud man's chin. She gathered all her courage and began to deepen another foothold in the wall. She had not taken three steps up when a mountain goat called from a rock above her.

"I see the buzzards shall soon have a meal," said the goat. "Tell me, why do you pick the hardest place to climb?"

"Do you know a better way?" asked Tokarra.

"I climb to the top every day," said the goat. "I will show you my way."

Tokarra followed as the goat walked a stony path that led up a gentle slope. The goat bounded ahead as Tokarra climbed behind. The path was strewn with tiny pebbles in many shapes and colors. As she climbed higher, the pebbles became stones with sharp edges. Tokarra lost her footing, cutting her bare knees and hands. Still, the path seemed easier than the cliff.

"We are almost to the top," called the goat.

Tokarra could see the summit. It was just past five more boulders.

Suddenly, rocks tumbled, dust flew, and the cliff thundered. The goat sprang out of the way as boulders crashed down all around it, flattening trees and bushes.

"Watch out!" warned the goat.

Tokarra turned and raced ahead of the tumbling rocks, her feet stumbling and sliding. She sat down and skidded to the ground at the base of the cliff. At last all of the boulders came to rest, some against masses of trees, others on the hard earth beside her.

Tokarra stood and brushed off her skinned legs. She let out a sigh. "It was a good path for a goat," she told herself, "but not for a human."

She studied the steep cliff and thought, as only a human can. She took off her sandals and put them in her net bag. Then, looping the bag over her shoulder, she dug out a foothold and began to climb the cliff.

Tokarra inched her way up, one foothold at a time. Her fingers and toes began to ache, then became numb. The wind stung her eyes. She cried silent tears.

As she reached the top, the limestone crumbled. Her small hands slipped. She nearly fell. She clutched the side of the cliff like a baby holding onto its mother.

Tokarra breathed deeply to stay calm. She saw a small hackberry tree whose branches hung near the edge. She moved closer, reaching across until her hand encircled a small branch. She tested it to see if it would hold. Then she seized the limb and pulled herself up over the ledge.

The snake and the goat, watching from the summit, stared at her in surprise.

"Mine was a good path for a human," Tokarra declared as she took out the tools to make a fire.

Tokarra knelt next to the signal hearth near the cliff's edge. She rolled the fire stick between her palms, making the stick spin. She blew softly on tiny embers that fell on the hearth stick, catching the kindling on fire. Her father and the clan would see her signal fire and know of her success.

She unbraided her long hair, and the wind caught it. She raised her arms. The wind swept through the canyons. "Tokarra!" it seemed to call. "Today, she becomes a woman."

The Speed Skater

By Katherine Howard

Rick Lang skated back and forth and around and around on the dark, shining surface of the frozen Pedera River in northern Alberta. Rick had been trying hard to be a really good, fast ice skater ever since he had moved from Texas. His father, who was an engineer, had been assigned a post at an oil company in the Canadian North.

"If you practice hard, Rick," said Mr. Reid, the Willowbend school principal, "you'll be able to play on the team. All you need is speed."

"And that," thought Rick grimly, "is hard to get."

Most of the Canadian boys had been ice-skating since they were small, but Rick, at eleven, hadn't skated at all until coming to Canada. So he practiced and practiced.

Today his parents were in the neighboring town of Carstairs for the afternoon. Rick decided he would skate up the river to see Doug Allen, his best friend. Doug's father was in the lumber business, about a mile from Rick's home.

Rick skated along in swift, gliding strokes, trying all the time to increase his speed. When, breathless, he reached the path up the riverbank leading to the Allens' house, he took off his skating boots, fastened them by their laces around his neck, and put on the moccasins he carried in his pocket. Then he walked up the path to the house.

He knocked at the door. There was no answer. Disappointed, Rick knocked harder. He thought he heard a muffled voice call something. He pushed open the door and went in.

Then he felt really scared. Doug lay on the floor. His right leg was strangely twisted and his face was a funny gray color. Faintly he said, "Rick, I need help. I thought no one would ever come."

As Rick bent over him, Doug groaned. "I fell off that ladder when I was trying to change the light-bulb on that ceiling lamp. Mom and Dad are away. My leg is broken." His voice trailed off.

Rick's face grew white, too. What could he do? He couldn't move Doug. He knew he shouldn't, anyway, until a doctor had seen him. Phone a doctor. That was the first thing. He stepped to the phone and cranked the handle rapidly.

Doug opened his eyes. "The phone's out," he said weakly. "Went dead this afternoon." He looked up at Rick, his eyes heavy and shadowed with pain. "Can you skate upriver to Fosters'? It's on a different line—their phone. Might be working." He closed his eyes again, clenched his fists, and set his teeth.

Rick's mind was racing. Even if the Fosters could help him, how could he leave Doug?

As if Doug knew his thoughts, he whispered, "I'll be all right. Only hurry! Hurry!"

Rick looked at his watch. It was five o'clock. He tore out of the house and down to the river. It was dark now, but the snow on the banks and a dim moon gave a little light. Frantically, Rick laced on his skating boots, then he was off, skating faster than he ever had before.

The river, under its thin covering of snow, looked grim and mysterious and lonely. Suddenly, from high up on the bank, came the chilling howl of a timber wolf, and from some distance away came an answering chorus of eerie howls.

Rick shivered. He didn't even have a flashlight. When he left home he had thought that Mrs. Allen would ask him to stay for supper and that Mr. Allen would drive him home. Now he was here in the middle of the river, in the dark, with wolves not far away.

Rick felt chilled to his toes. Then he thought of Doug, lying hurt and helpless. He skated on. He knew he couldn't keep up that wild pace, so he slowed up a little. Then Rick saw something ahead. He stared, terrified. Stretching from bank to bank, was a channel of black water.

"Water!" he gasped aloud. "Water, not ice!"

He felt sick and dazed. Bewildered, Rick passed a fur-mittened hand over his eyes. He had to get help. Suddenly he knew what he had to do.

Rick took a deep, deep breath. With a burst of speed, he surged forward—and sprang. He soared over the channel, landing within two feet of the water's edge. Rick shuddered, fell onto his knees, and felt a sharp pain tear through his kneecap. But he was up in a moment, skimming over the silent river in rapid, swooping strides.

An owl hooted. There was a sudden shrill scream from the dark shadow of a spruce.

Would he never see the lights of the Foster house? Had he passed it somewhere back in the shadows? Suppose there was nobody home? Or suppose he couldn't get Doctor Denny?

He shook himself angrily. No use thinking thoughts like that. He had to get to the Fosters'.

His legs felt as if they were made of solid clay. But he pushed them, one in front of the other, skating on and on.

Suddenly he was there. Above him, on the left were the lights of a house. He almost collapsed on the bank. Quickly he took off his boots, hung them around his neck, took his moccasins from his pocket, and dragged himself wearily up the snowy slope to the house.

He staggered into the living room without knocking. He felt strangely lightheaded. Through a mist he saw Mrs. Foster staring at him.

"The doctor!" His voice was barely a whisper. "Get Doctor Denny, please. Doug Allen's hurt!"

The room seemed to be going dark around him. Someone gripped his shoulder. It was Mr. Foster. Everything was foggy. Then Mr. Foster handed Rick a glass of something hot and comforting. He began to feel better.

Turning from the phone, Mrs. Foster said, "Doctor Denny is on his way."

Rick sighed. "There was only Doug there," he said. "He was lying on the floor, and his leg was twisted. The phone was out. It was five o'clock when I left, but I lost time at the channel." Seeing the wondering expression on Mr. Foster's face, Rick told about the wide channel of water across the river. "I thought I was licked then," he said, "but I knew I had to make it."

47

Mr. Foster looked at his watch. Then he said, "Rick, you had to put on your skates and take them off, climb up and down the riverbank, skate around all those curves, and it's now only twenty minutes after five." He was quiet for a minute. Then, his eyes twinkling, he said, "You know, Rick, you might be the fastest boy on skates in Willowbend school. Perhaps we should let Mr. Reid know about this. I'll bet he'll be glad to have you on the speed-skating team.

He patted Rick on the back, "You did a wonderful thing tonight, Rick, for your friend. We're proud of you. Now, come on, speed skater, I'll drive you home."

Rick got up. He felt fine. He wasn't even tired. Doug would be all right. Mr. Foster was going to stop at the Allens' to make sure. And Rick was a speed skater!

The Shortcut

By Paul A. Witty

Spring vacation! Lisa could think of nothing else on the last Friday before vacation. She came running downstairs to have breakfast. It was a beautiful sunny day in early April. She looked out the dining room window. Yellow jonquils lined the walk. Forsythia bushes along the white fence brightened the landscape with glowing golden blossoms. A robin was moving slowly across the lawn. Lisa's mother said, "Isn't this a beautiful day? Our jonquils and tulips are out, and the forsythia was never so beautiful."

"Yes, Mom," Lisa answered. "I know it is a fine day. But I hoped it might be snowing."

Her mom laughed. "There's no chance, Lisa. We've had an early spring. But don't worry, there'll be plenty of snow in Colorado, and you can ski as much as you wish. I had a letter from your aunt Emma in Boulder last week. She said that the skiing is still wonderful. Her whole family is looking forward to our visit next week. It's too bad your dad has to go to Texas on business."

"Yeah," Lisa answered. "It's hard to believe we'll be in Boulder Sunday night. Isn't that great?"

Mrs. Grant remarked, "The first time I went to Boulder, the trip took two days and a night on the train. Now Boulder's only a few hours from Indiana by plane."

Late Sunday night Lisa and her mother arrived in Boulder. Lisa looked at the clear sky. The stars seemed so near, she felt she could touch them.

They were greeted by Aunt Emma and her twelve-year-old son, Bill, who was almost Lisa's age. Lisa looked at the sky again.

"I don't think it's going to snow. There isn't a cloud in the sky," she said skeptically.

"You're right, Lisa. It's clear now. But the evening paper predicts a heavy snow for tomorrow," her aunt explained.

Everyone was up early Monday morning. A light snow was falling gently. The morning passed rapidly as they prepared for skiing. After lunch, Lisa, her aunt, and her cousin Bill started for the slope twenty miles away. Lisa's mother preferred to stay home. She said she would have dinner ready when they returned.

The skiers soon reached the resort at the foot of the slope and got ready for the ascent. On a new, fast-moving lift, they were hoisted quickly to the top. Below, everything was white. An occasional skier could be seen sliding down the slope almost like a giant bird with huge feet.

Lisa's Aunt Emma was the first to start down the slope. Then Bill followed, and finally Lisa. All of them glided down and landed safely. The hours passed so quickly that it was almost time to go home before they realized it. The snow continued to fall. As a wind arose, Lisa's aunt became a little concerned and said, "Perhaps we should start home before dusk."

"One more run," Lisa begged. And Bill urged his mother to let them stay a little longer.

Soon they were at the top of the incline again. Lisa's aunt led once more, and Bill followed. Now it was Lisa's turn. As she was sailing along, she thought, "I'll take that shortcut near the end of the slope and surprise Bill and Aunt Emma by getting to the bottom first."

The snow was almost blinding, yet Lisa could recognize the familiar signs. She was sure she'd know the place to turn off. Yet she was doubtful shortly after she had made the turn. It was only a few moments later that she knew for certain she was on the wrong path. The landscape suddenly grew unfamiliar and the path became very rough. Lisa stopped abruptly and peered through the blinding snow. She could see nothing but snow in all directions. However, she was just able to make out in the distance the outline of a large boulder almost entirely covered with snow.

Fright seized her in the realization that she was lost in a raging snowstorm. She called loudly. There was no answer. She called still louder, her voice trembling this time. Again there was no answer, only a faint echo of her voice.

Panic was about to grip her. Suddenly she remembered Ms. Wright, her Girl Scout leader, saying, "In a great difficulty, don't panic!" Ms. Wright had told the troop about a girl whose calmness saved her from drowning. And she had described another Scout who had built a refuge in the snow and had stayed there until rescuers came. Lisa called out again. Then she looked around, thinking, "How can I make a shelter?"

Lisa went over to some nearby pine trees and cut off the low branches with her knife. At last she had a large number of branches. The snow, by this time, had piled up on the north and west sides of the boulder. On the east the boulder gave some protection from the wind, and the surrounding snow was firmer on this side, too. Lisa slowly dug into the snow, rounding out a small shelter that opened toward the east. She pulled the branches one by one into the shelter, and lined its walls. She kept a few extra branches to cover the opening and to use as a bed.

Lisa was startled suddenly as she thought she heard a dog barking. Pushing aside the branches, she put her head out and called. But there was no answer. She called again, and then crawled back into the shelter and lay down. She was very tired. What a relief! She was surprised at how comfortable she was. Soon she was sound asleep.

After what seemed like several hours later, Lisa was awakened by the barking of dogs and the sound of her name being called. She drew back the branches from her snug retreat and looked out. The sun was shining brightly and the snow sparkled like gems. She called, and this time her calls were answered. Soon Lisa was surrounded by Bill, her father, her aunt, and neighborhood friends.

Her father held Lisa in his arms and said, "Thank God you're safe!"

"Where did you come from, Dad?" Lisa asked. "I thought you were in Texas."

"I took a plane late last night and arrived at daybreak. Your mother telephoned and said you were lost—that three search parties were looking for you. About one o'clock they returned. They had had no response to their calls, the flares, and their other efforts to locate you. I guess you couldn't see the flares or hear their voices."

"No, Dad, I didn't see anything. Once, early last night, I thought I heard barking. I called out but no one answered. Then after I had made my shelter, I lay down. It was nice and warm. I was so comfortable, I went to sleep."

Mr. Grant examined the snug shelter admiringly. "Lisa, why did you think of making it?"

"Well, Dad, last winter at a Girl Scout meeting, Ms. Wright warned us to keep calm if we were in great danger. And she told us how to make a snug shelter to protect us in storms. I'll never forget her saying, 'Remember, in an emergency don't panic. You can almost always find a way out of danger if you keep calm!'"

"Everyone ought to remember that good advice. I am very proud of you, Lisa."

Suddenly Bill ran up, carrying the skis that Lisa had abandoned the night before. "I found them under the snow about fifty feet away," he said. "They're good as new. Let's ski down."

"I'll go with you," said Lisa's dad.

"That's great," she said happily.

"I'll go with you, too," Bill said. "And I have some advice for you, Lisa. Don't take any short-cuts this time."

Clam Tide

By Kristine L. Franklin

"Clam tide!" my brother yelled as he leaped out of bed and threw on his clothes. I got up and peeked out the window. The water was so far out that it looked like a shiny silver line far beyond the beach.

"Can I go?" I asked, stifling a yawn and trying hard to look wide awake.

"Naw," he said. He laced up his old tennis shoes. "It's hard work, and you're too little." The door banged as he rushed out.

"Mama-a-a!" I hollered in my saddest voice.

"Kelly won't take me clam digging." I started to cry because I was disappointed, but mostly because I was mad at my brother.

Soon I was following him down to the tide flats. I had to walk fast, because now my brother was mad at me. He swung the bucket in one hand and held the clam shovel in the other, and I could tell by the way he took giant steps that he wished I was home. But Mom had said I could go.

"Hurry up," he said, without turning around. "The tide won't stay out all day, you know." When we got to the edge of the beach, the ground was covered with rocks and smelled like rotten seaweed and dead barnacles. We hiked down the slope toward the water.

Beyond the rocky beach the tide flats were muddy. It was the oozy kind of mud that sucks off your shoes if you stand too long in one place. I had a hard time hurrying through that stuff, and so did Kelly. Once, he had to stop and slowly, carefully pull his foot up so he wouldn't lose a shoe. I giggled at the sound it made coming out. My brother gave me a nasty look.

After that his feet kept getting stuck, so he tried tiptoeing across the mud. Next he tried hopping. Then he tried running fast with little tiny steps. I followed him, imitating everything he did.

By the time we got to the clam-digging place, we were covered with blobs and splatters and teeny freckles of stinky black mud. My side hurt. I don't know if it was from running or from too much laughing.

Kelly put one foot on the clam shovel and pushed it hard into the mud. "When I bring up a shovelful, your job is to look for clams." Kelly liked to give me jobs. He heaved a pile of sandy muck toward me. It plopped all over my shoes.

I stuck my hands into the mess and began feeling for the hard little clams. "Got one!" I said. I rinsed off my prize in clean salt water. Kelly kept digging and plopping down the piles.

Clam by clam, the bucket began to fill. I was choosy about which ones to keep. If they were too big or too little, I tossed them into the shallow water nearby. The big ones splashed my brother.

"How many clams is that?" Kelly asked as he flung down an especially gooey load.

"Fifty-three," I said. There was a rule that each person could take only thirty clams a day, so I was counting them. I felt through the new pile for a few more.

Now I was kneeling in three inches of water, separating clams from rocks as fast as I could. "The tide is coming in," I said. My brother pretended to ignore me, but worked a little faster. His feet and legs were sunk down into the mud, and it made him look short. The water in the hole he had made was getting deeper.

"That's sixty," I said, tossing the last clam into the bucket. "Thirty for you, thirty for me. Let's go." I looked at my big brother and realized he was scared. *Very* scared.

"I'm stuck," he said, trying to sound brave.

"Pull one foot up and then the other." The water around my own ankles made me nervous.

"I already tried it." He squirmed and tried it again. The more he moved, the deeper he went.

"Dig in your shovel and pull yourself out," I said. He tried it. The shovel fell over.

"It's too mushy. It won't work!" He didn't sound brave anymore. I looked around frantically for firm ground away from the hole and the loose mud. I wished I was big enough to pull him out. I wished it was me who was stuck instead of him.

A few feet away, the ground wasn't as gooey. The water came to just above my ankles. I quickly skinned off my jeans and stood there in my bathing suit.

"What are you doing? Are you crazy?" Now my brother's voice sounded funny. He was crying. I threw him the legs of my jeans.

"You pull on that end, and I'll pull on this end." I took hold of the top end.

"You're not strong enough!" he cried. "I'll pull you over." But then he tried. I didn't fall over. I sank down in the mud.

"Keep pulling!" I screamed at him.

It took awhile, but soon I could see it was working. Kelly was climbing hand over hand up my jeans and out of his hole, and I was sinking farther into mine. I held on. The water crept up around my hips.

"Yahhhh!" Kelly yelled as he pulled free. He scrambled up and got his footing. He took two big splashing steps and stood above me. "It's OK. Don't be scared."

My brother grabbed me under the arms and pulled so hard it hurt. For one horrible second, nothing happened. Then the mud let go.

He lifted me up and hugged me. He pressed his cheek against mine, and all our tears and dirty freckles smeared together. "Let's get away from here," he said. He carried me out of the water and beyond the reach of the tide.

Kelly put me down gently and started across the flats. This time I didn't walk behind him, and we didn't hurry. The bucket, the shovel, the clams, my jeans—all were lost and forgotten.

We didn't talk much on the way home, but we squeezed hands a couple of times and grinned a lot. Whenever one of our feet got stuck in the mud, we laughed together at the funny sound it made coming out.

Chanook and the Caribou Calf

By Nadina Newman Marteny

On other days Chanook's mind would have been brimming with secrets, thoughts, and questions. Today, however, he thought of the letter from his new pen pal in New York City. She and Chanook had only their age in common—twelve years. Beyond that, their lives were foreign to one another. Chanook wanted to impress Nancy with as much exciting news as her first letter had held for him. The Eskimo boy thought this was not going to be possible. Her letter told of football games, her school play, movies, restaurants, and a wonderful place called Central Park.

Chanook's younger sister, Neevee, squirmed on a rock ledge beside him at his favorite fishing spot. Chanook had told her to sit quietly. Fishing and thinking were his objectives, not baby-sitting. He hoped to solve his problem and carry home many silvery fish to eat. But Neevee chattered and wiggled like a fuzzy bear cub, making Chanook's task difficult.

A herd of caribou began crossing the river not far from them. Suddenly, Chanook's keen, dark eyes caught a frantic movement in the ice-choked water. He scrambled to his feet. Only a short distance away, a nearly drowned young caribou calf was struggling to reach shore.

"Neevee, look! That calf is going to drown!" Chanook yelled "We have to help him!"

Chanook stood at the water's edge. "I'm a good swimmer," he thought, "but not good enough to pull the calf out of the water." He knew the throbbing river could easily suck him into its swirling current. Then he saw the fishnet lying on the ledge next to him. Sometimes they used the large net for salmon, or to carry a big catch home on the dog sled.

"Neevee, help me with this net," he instructed as he pulled open the top of the net. "I'm going to throw it over the calf. The minute it settles on top of him, pull these cords to draw the net around him."

Neevee was small, but she was strong and had helped her mother with the fishing nets before. She knew how to pull the net cords together to make the net into a sac. But never before did she have such a large catch.

"But, Chanook," she protested, "even when the net is around him, the pull of the river will be too strong. We could lose the calf and our net in the rushing current!"

"No," he said, glancing around him. "First, we have to anchor the net to something very strong. Then I'll be able to pull him in a little at a time."

Neevee and Chanook found a huge rock not far from where they were standing. "That's where you'll have to wrap the end of the net," Chanook said. "And you'll have to be quick!"

The calf was scared when the net closed in around him. He struggled against it, but Neevee had already wrapped the cords tightly around the rock. Though the calf was heavy, Chanook drew in the net hand over hand. At last the calf reached the land. Chanook carefully pulled the net away from the calf, who lay shaking and breathing heavily on the rocky shore.

"Wow, that was too close," Chanook crooned to the caribou calf.

"He's safe now, thanks to us, but what are we going to do with him?" Neevee asked.

"Dad will know what to do—and he'll be surprised when he sees our catch!" said Chanook.

Dad was a short distance downriver from the children. He, too, was fishing. His lure hit the water just as Chanook and Neevee hurried to his side. Chanook spurted out the story of the daring rescue. "Will the mother caribou be able to find the calf, Dad?" Chanook asked.

"Take the calf to the riverbank, to where you first saw it, Chanook," Dad suggested. "Don't worry, son, the cow will find her calf. She will search for him until the herd begins to move away," he concluded reassuringly. "Neevee and I will go back home now. We'll be waiting to hear what happens."

Chanook and the calf quickly reached their destination at the river's edge. Chanook felt relief as he untied the rope from around the calf's neck and set him free. "You must wait here for your mother, little calf," he ordered softly.

Chanook's dark, warm eyes were solemn as he hid himself nearby behind a huge pile of rocks. His thoughts raced with fears for the calf's future. The calf must be so afraid. Chanook thought now of how he had felt only moments before, longing for excitement. Now he wished for that quiet.

Almost in reply to Chanook's worst thoughts, a half-grown grizzly bear lumbered out of the thick underbrush. The caribou calf stood motionless.

Finally, the bear spotted the defenseless calf. Chanook's heart leaped to his throat. The calf stiffened but was too tired to try an escape. The fat, shaggy bear sniffed the air with a long, jerky swing of its massive head. It bounced on its thick front paws. Just as the bear began to lunge for the calf, the mother caribou came running. Her big rounded hooves pounded on the soggy earth. The bear jumped back.

"Am I glad to see that calf's mother," thought Chanook, quietly watching from his hiding place.

The cow spread her great cinnamon-brown legs. All four powerful hoofs were planted firmly on the ground. She held her head low and looked as though she dared the bear to come forward.

"That grizzly is no match for a mad cow. It had better run if it knows what's good for it," Chanook thought.

Wisely, the terrified bear backed down the river's slippery edge. A safe distance from the fierce glare of the cow, the grizzly turned and disappeared into the haven of the woods. Cautiously, the cow moved toward her shivering calf. She signaled him to follow by bobbing her great head. Together, the two quickly made their way along the river's bank, out of Chanook's sight.

"They're on their way to join their herd," thought Chanook happily. He was thinking of the massive migrating caribou herd that he had seen earlier in the day. Chanook's chest swelled with pride and happiness. He rose slowly, trying not to break what seemed to be a magic spell. A short distance away he located his fishing gear. He had no fish to show for his adventure-filled day. But somehow that didn't seem to matter. He had something more important. A newfound pride.

Chanook headed toward his village. Dusk was closing in quickly, and the dark golden sun was busy dropping behind the muted rose-colored mountains. The sky was filled with colors of violet, gold, and shimmering pink. The twinkling stars matched Chanook's spirit. Close by, the boy could see the warm, inviting lights of his small village home. The tiny frame house welcomed him. After his meal he would write Nancy of the day's wonders and of the quiet times, too.

Chanook had a warm feeling deep inside. It was good to have his family, home, and friends. Like the caribou's, Chanook's wilderness life was not easy, but it was a very special way to live.

Rock Hound Hideout

By Mary Etta Logan

"Oops!" Kerry Lane clung to the snaggy branches of the scrub oak. Rocks and gravel slid down the slope below. After a moment she pulled herself up beside the shrub and breathed deeply of the pine-scented mountain air. She was glad to be back again on her uncle's ranch where she had spent so many happy summers.

"Guess I'd better watch the trail instead of looking so far ahead," she said to herself, wondering why she couldn't locate the large "throne rock."

Climbing swiftly, Kerry soon reached the tall pine. Now it was but a few steps to the big rock. After rounding the last thick clump of brush, she stopped suddenly.

"What! Where!" she exclaimed. No wonder she hadn't seen the throne rock—it was gone!

Just then Kerry saw a black-bearded stranger, staggering under the weight of a big sack. He was coming slowly toward her. Quickly Kerry crouched behind some brush. She heard the stranger puffing as he came nearer. Turning sharply, Kerry saw the big hole where the throne rock had been. When she glanced back, she found the man had disappeared.

"A cave!" Kerry whispered. "And that stranger! What's going on here?"

There was only one way to find out. A shiver of fear raced up and down Kerry's spine as she decided to follow and investigate. There was not time to return to the ranch for help. Maybe this man was alone. On the other hand, the cave might be a hideout for thieves.

Questions raced through her mind. Who was the stranger? What was in the sack?

Kerry moved forward slowly. A twig snapped underfoot. She froze into a motionless crouch, then she moved forward very slowly until she reached the opening. Quickly she slipped inside. Keeping one hand on the rough rock wall, Kerry crept silently along in the darkness. After some fifteen feet of groping, she felt a sudden sharp turn in the wall. Rounding it cautiously, she heard voices. They sounded excited. She couldn't turn back now.

Kerry's soft-soled shoes made no noise as she edged forward. Then she saw a lighted lantern swinging from the ceiling of a large circular room. Some men were sitting around a rough plank table. In the center of the table was the sack the stranger had been carrying. Kerry couldn't see what was in the sack, but she heard low voices and snatches of a conversation.

"This one's a beauty—the best we've taken. Here's another fine specimen. This is real treasure."

Kerry's heart sank. She was sure she had stumbled onto a gang of robbers. Jewel thieves, she guessed, from the occasional glitter of reflected light given off by small objects on the table. She counted five people and knew there was one other. Six to one—and no way to defend herself!

As Kerry slowly turned back, she heard a movement. Whirling, she saw someone coming toward her. She dropped to the floor and flattened herself behind a big boulder. If only the person would go back to the table — but, no, the person was coming straight toward Kerry's hiding place! Knowing she would be discovered, Kerry sprang to her feet. The other stopped quickly in surprise.

"Who are you?" he asked. He was a boy, not much older than Kerry herself.

"I'm Kerry Lane from the Lazy L. Ranch in the valley below," Kerry replied. "And who are you, and why are you hiding on my uncle's ranch?"

"I'm Paul Morgan," the boy answered as he turned to the others. "Dad, this is Kerry Lane." Then he introduced Kerry to everyone else.

Kerry glanced from one to another in bewilderment. They didn't act like thieves!

"I'm Professor Morgan from the university," the older man explained. "These are students from my geology class. We're all rock hounds. Your uncle gave us permission to use this cave."

"Rock hounds!" Kerry exclaimed in an astonished voice.

On the table gleamed and sparkled a pile of brightly colored rocks that had been emptied out of the sack.

"What on earth do you do with them? They're just rocks, aren't they?" Kerry asked.

"Dad is making a collection for the university," Paul replied. "He wants more of the crystals, such as amethyst, beryl, and aragonite — like these." He pointed to certain rocks. "In the evening, while the others sort and label the best specimens, I use the discards to make gifts."

On the table nearby was a group of trays, paperweights, and jewel settings, ground and polished. As Kerry touched the stones, she decided she, too, would like to be a rock hound.

"If you've lived around here, perhaps you know where we might find some really fine specimens," Paul remarked.

"I think I do," Kerry said. "I've wandered over these hills every summer since I was six. I've seen a lot of rocks like those you have, but I didn't know they were good for anything. I'll be glad to take you to explore Red Rock Canyon tomorrow if you like."

So it was agreed.

Later, as Kerry returned to the ranch house, she whistled gaily. Maybe she hadn't exposed the hideout of a gang of jewel thieves. But she had made some new friends—and some discoveries, too. She was sure of a good summer ahead.

Rough Water

By Gordon H. Messegee

Clyde and I didn't believe Pete when he warned us that a storm was coming. It was true that the wet, gray clouds had already reached the hills and were piling up back over the Sound. And the sea-green firs were starting their weaving battle with the March wind. But we didn't want to believe Pete. We were going camping.

Besides, it was only six miles from Sandy Point to Kemas Island. Usually the crossing is simple, except in the early spring when the Sada current runs strong. The Sada runs west by north and about halfway between the Point and the Island. Greenhorns, frequently misjudging it, wind up past the Island and in the center of the wide strait that leads to the ocean. Today the current was not only strong but off its course. We could tell that by the broken branches and the driftwood that raced by in the cold, whitecapped water.

We piled our camping gear into the *Sea Sprite* (that's the name of the boat we own together), careful to balance it well. Pete stood by on the dock, watching us.

"It's too rough out there. You hadn't oughter go today," he warned.

"Don't worry, Pete, we'll make it. We've been raised on the Sound. We're old sea dogs." Clyde laughed good-naturedly.

As usual, when Clyde is for a thing, I am, too. Clyde and I are cousins, the same age. We are always together, and couldn't think more of each other if we were brothers.

Pete didn't say anything more as we shoved off and raced downstream. At the oars, Clyde was directing the *Sea Sprite* to head northeast to cut the Sada. Clyde rowed more than halfway. He's always like that.

Then we changed places, being careful to balance the *Sea Sprite* against the roll. Now we were beginning to head into a strange swell that seemed out of proportion to the force of the wind. Clyde sat at the stern and bailed. I lined up his head with Sandy Point and started to row. At first it felt good—the tough resistance of the oars, and the tease of the waves as they tried to jerk us off our course. Rowing into them gave you a feeling of power.

Soon I noticed it was getting darker than it should be for late afternoon. Glancing behind me, I could just make out the bulge of Becker's Rock. The cave, our destination, was just to the left. Then came a lull in the wind. A big black cloud pressed down. Raindrops began to fall. And suddenly it became very dark. Clyde and I looked at each other. I was scared. I couldn't tell what Clyde was thinking.

The wind came back. Now it was north by west—cold and strong, and growing stronger. It snatched my hat and whipped at my jacket. It wrestled with the blades of the oars, making me fight to keep my seat. Clyde shouted something about changing places with me, but I pretended not to hear. It was my turn to row. Soon we couldn't have changed places if we had tried. Swift waves began to reach for the gunwale. Each time our roll caught them the wrong way, water rushed in. I could feel it cold against my ankles.

I had nothing to steer by, now that Sandy Point was lost in the darkness. All I could do was try to keep the *Sea Sprite* from swamping, and try to guess the right direction. I had to meet each wave just right, on the corner of the bow—a few inches this way or that and we would be gone.

I could see Clyde hunched over as he bailed faster and faster—scrape-bang, scrape-bang, scrape-bang!

My feet grew numb, and my arms and back ached with the cold and strain. Suddenly I felt scared, more scared than I had ever been in all my life. I was afraid we were back in the Sada and were being carried out to sea. And that would be the end. Fear, like some horrible monster, gripped me in its clutch so that I couldn't move. I started to cry.

Then I heard Clyde calling to me. "I'm sick, Budd, awfully sick. I can't bail anymore."

Once in a while Clyde had these spells—nervous chills, the doctor called them. He'd outgrow them, the doctor said.

"Take it easy, Clyde. Try to hold steady. We'll be out of this mess soon," I shouted, and found my voice wasn't even trembling.

Suddenly the awful fear that I had thought would overpower me a moment before loosened its hold. Something bigger and stronger had taken over. My whole being was filled with just one thought: I had to get Clyde safely to shore. I was able to row stronger now, ship less water, judge the distance better. Then all at once I could see the outline of Becker's Rock. We were only a hundred yards to the lee of the cave!

Later that night the moon came out, full and round and wonderful, shining down on Clyde and me as we lay snugly wrapped in our blankets in front of a roaring fire. Clyde was feeling better now, still shaky, but himself again.

"We wouldn't be here, Budd, if it wasn't for you. I'll never . . . "

I didn't want him to say anything more about it, at least not now. So I broke in, trying to make a joke of things. "I was so scared about you, Clyde, that I didn't have any scare left for the storm."

But inside I couldn't think of anything but how thankful I was that we had both made it through the rough water to solid land.

Suli's Bravery

By Ruth Bishop Juline

Suli held tightly to her brother as the pony carried them across the sand wash and away from their hogan. She was starting her sixth spring, and it was time that she learned how to look after the sheep and goats. Someday, when eleven-year-old Joe left the reservation to attend school, she would be left to care for the flocks alone.

The goats hurried ahead, pushing against one another. But the sheep moved more slowly, eating every blade of grass. Once in a while Suli shook her can of stones to hurry the slow-moving ones along. The sharp-pointed hoofs of the animals left tracks in the sand as the flocks made their way to a water hole. Here they bunched together, dipping their woolly faces into the water.

The children rested while the animals drank. Suli, who had always stayed close to the hogan, looked about at the miles of land surrounding her.

"The world is so big, and I am so small," she thought to herself.

Suli imagined the time when she would come alone to the water hole. Would she be wise and unafraid? Joe was. And her brother was strong. The muscles of his arms were like leather thongs.

When the sun was high in the sky, Joe drove the flocks farther along to a hilly spot covered with patches of green grass. The animals grazed quietly. Joe stretched himself on the ground, his black broad-brimmed hat shading his eyes. He sang softly the high-pitched song of the shepherds. Suli sat beside him, her feet drawn under her.

As the hours dragged by and the sun slid across the western sky, the children played games with small pebbles.

Suddenly, Suli looked up. "There goes Garnet!" she cried. "And taking her little one with her!"

Joe was on his feet at once. "The troublemaker," he cried. "She has no fear. Come, we must bring her back at once."

He knew this country as well he knew his own face. The hill, so round on this side, was a steep cliff on the far side.

Helping his sister onto the pony, Joe swung into the saddle and whirled the animal toward the straying goats. But before he could head them off, the curious kid ventured too far and went tumbling over the brink.

The children were on the ground before the pony slid to a stop. They dashed to the edge of the cliff.

"Is he hurt?" Suli whispered.

"I can't see him." Joe's eyes searched the gorge.

Cautiously, Suli flattened herself on a rock that jutted farther than the rest. She strained to see any movement below.

Baa-aa! The pitiful sound reached her ears.

"There he is!" she cried, pointing.

The little kid, trembling and frightened, huddled on a flat rock ledge where he had landed when he fell.

Joe stared at the perilous sight. "How can we get to him?" he puzzled. "The wall is solid rock and straight down." He reached for the coil of rope on the saddle horn, then shook his head. "A lasso would choke him," he decided.

The mother goat, wild-eyed and excited, ran along the edge, bleating sounds of comfort to her kid. In the lowland the flocks milled restlessly, eager to return to the night corral. Shadows of cacti were lengthening like strange, stiff fingers. Joe and Suli knew that soon the helpless kid would be easy prey for hungry wild animals.

"Let me down," Suli cried suddenly. "I am small. The rope will hold me and the little one, too."

For a brief moment her brother hesitated, then he sprang into action. Tying one end of the rope under Suli's arms and the other around the saddle horn, he began lowering the child to the ledge.

"Be brave," he whispered at the sight of her pale face. "The pony will hold you tight." But he sent up a fervent prayer that the rope would be steady and his arms strong.

Below, with her feet safely on the ledge, Suli spoke softly to the trembling kid, "Quiet, little one. Suli will take you to your mother."

From above, Joe watched every move. He held tight to the rope, no longer taut.

Gathering the kid into her arms, Suli cried, "Pull!"

The rope tightened as Joe urged the pony to take one step—two steps—three. Suli's body swung free, and she felt herself being hauled up. She looked down, and sickening fear filled her. If the rope broke, she would go hurtling to the rocky bottom.

The kid, helpless in her grip, felt like lead in her arms. The rope cut into her body, and jagged rocks tore at her clothes. But at last she was near the top. Joe quickly took the kid from her, then dragged her over the edge. In a moment the rope was slipped from her body.

"You were very brave, little sister!" her brother said proudly.

"Someday, will I be a good shepherd?"

"The very best!" Joe said.

Adventure of the Footprints

By Elizabeth Rainbow

Keith picked up a handful of snow. "Just right for skiing," he said, tossing it toward his sister and his two best friends, Dan and Dave Granger, who were toiling up the hill behind him.

"Yeah, skiing will be great today," Judy retorted "*if* we ever get to the top of this hill!"

The hill was not steep, but it was covered with deep, powdery snow. On the other side was the old Karlsted place, an abandoned estate with a long, sloping front lawn, where the children could practice skiing.

As they neared the top, Keith suddenly stopped. "Look!" he exclaimed, pointing to a shining red car parked just outside the stone wall surrounding the old estate.

"Wow! What a car!" Dan said.

"I wonder whose it is?" asked Judy. "Must belong to some tourist."

Keith laughed. "A tourist up on this hill in the winter?" He shook his head. "I don't think a tourist would be interested in the old Karlsted place. No one has lived in that house for the last twenty years. Dad says that after Mr. Karlsted was killed in an accident, his wife and their young son moved back to Sweden to live. Ever since then the house has been empty. Empty and gone to ruin."

"But here are some fresh tracks going through the gates toward the house." Dan pointed to what looked like a man's footprints.

"You're right, Dan. Someone has been here. Let's see if we can find out who it is." Dave was already running on ahead, and the rest followed him through the sagging gates and up the snow-covered path.

Soon they came in sight of the old ruin. It was a square wooden structure with a huge porch. The darkened windows stared empily across the sloping yard. At the end of the yard was a stone wall, and beyond it was a steep half-mile-long hill that ran down the valley to the town of Lakeville.

The children followed the footprints across the yard to the crumbling porch and a doorless opening in the front of the house. They peered inside.

A strong scent of rotting wood and musty plaster came from the dank interior. The doorway was blocked by a great heap of broken laths, rotting beams, and crumbled plaster. The air was full of thick dust.

"The ceiling must have just come down." Dave pointed upward. "Lucky we weren't under it, or we'd have been pinned down for good."

Then the children heard a faint groan. It came from the heap of plaster and wood.

Keith's face paled. He darted toward the heap. "We've got to clear away this stuff!" he cried. "There's someone pinned under it."

Everyone worked fast. Soon their ski clothes were white with plaster dust and their hands black with ancient dirt.

"I need help," Judy shouted. "I can't move this thing an inch."

A heavy, rotted beam was wedged tightly between the walls, and there was another one beneath it.

"I don't think we'll be able to move 'em," grunted Dave.

"Besides, if we move this one, it could cause more of the ceiling or wall to come down." said Dan.

Keith looked grim. "We'll have to get help right away," he said.

"How? Where?" Judy spun toward him. "We've got to get it quickly."

"It would take almost an hour to get back to Lakeville by the cleared road," reminded Dan.

Dave nodded. "And the snow on the slope is too deep for our legs."

"Not with skis." Keith was already outside the doorway. "I can be down in Lakeville in minutes with these!" he called back.

Judy and the twins stared at him in horror. "You mean you're going to ski down that steep hill on the other side of the wall? You'll break your neck."

Keith's face was pale but determined. "It's the only way we can get help in time. I think I can do it, but I have to go right now."

"I'm going with you," Judy said. "If one of us falls, the other can go on." Her voice trembled, but she clamped on her skis just the same.

"Good idea! Dan, you and Dave hold the fort," Keith called out. Then he and Judy were away and over the rim of the hill.

Judy's heart was in her mouth as she started her downward descent. Trees rushed by her. Branches grabbed at her legs and arms. Her face began to freeze, and her eyes blurred. Hazily she saw Keith forge ahead, watched him almost topple and then regain his balance. Now the roofs of Lakeville were shooting up toward them like rockets. Panic clutched at Judy's throat.

Then the slope suddenly ended. She and Keith were moving swiftly across the valley floor and up to the door of Ed Greely's garage.

Minutes later they were in Ed Greely's truck, racing up the cleared road with the Lakeville Hospital ambulance behind them.

"Why, that's the ice skater's car!" exclaimed Ed as they pulled into the driveway. They jumped from the truck. The paramedics followed.

"I know that car belongs to Lennart Karlsted, the famous figure skater." Ed went on. "He bought gas from me this morning. He told me he was old Karlsted's son and had come back here to build a winter sports club on the site of the old property. It's to have ski runs, a skating rink—the works!"

Dan and Dave came running to meet them. "He's still alive!" they shouted. "We just heard him groan again."

The paramedics were able to pull the wreckage away and get the man safely out of the house and into the ambulance. The children watched as the ambulance drove away, hoping that Lennart Karlsted was going to be all right.

Later that evening, the children stopped by the hospital to see him. He was doing well, with only a great bruise on his forehead and his arm in a sling to show for his accident.

"Thanks to all of you I'm not worse off," he said, smiling at them from the hospital bed. "To you, my courageous friends, I owe my life. When I open my new club, I want you to know that you are always welcome there. To prove my word, I want to give each of you a lifelong membership."

He reached for a folder by his bed and took out four newly printed membership certificates, one for each child.

"Now we can really learn to ski," said Judy to Keith, her eyes shining with delight.

"I think you must be pretty good already," remarked Lennart Karlsted. "Didn't they tell me that both of you skied all the way down that steep hill to town?"

"Yeah! You should have seem them!" said Dan and Dave, gazing proudly at Judy and Keith. Then they turned to their new friend and started telling him the whole story.

The Storm

By Barbee Oliver Carleton

Annie ran all the way home from school. Overhead the sky loomed as gray as the sea.

"It's coming, Mom!" she shouted, slamming the door. "Everyone downtown says the winds have changed their course and we're in for a big storm after all!"

Her mother hurried into the kitchen, anxiety lining her face. "The news reporters say it will strike here around suppertime."

Annie noticed the oilskins she was wearing.

"You going out hauling with Dad? With a big storm coming?" Annie asked.

Her mother shook her head. "The ferry has stopped running because of the storm, so Dad can't get back from the mainland. This time, Annie, it's going to be up to us."

Hastily, her mother pulled on her high boots.

Growing up on an island, Annie knew better than to waste words. Storms gave warning, often with little time to spare. Then the islanders hurried to run their trap lines, to take care of their gear before the storm struck.

Annie's mother quickly made her a sandwich while Annie struggled into oilskins. Her head was whirling. Two hundred traps. Six to eight hours' hauling, usually. But they had only half the time!

Her mother's voice was level. "I can manage the boat. You'll have to handle the winch and haul as many traps as we have time for."

Thoughtfully, Annie dragged on her boots. "We'll take up just the traps near the ledges and leave the ones in deep water. This storm isn't a northeaster. More of a surface blow."

Her mother smiled. "We'll do fine, Annie."

Then Annie cried, "Oh, no! I forgot about the teacher, Mom. She's due here for supper!"

Several of the islander students were taking turns entertaining the teacher in their homes since she was a new teacher and an outsider from the mainland. "It was a way to make her stay on the island more pleasant and make her feel included," they said.

"But now," Annie sighed, "we won't be back in time to get her a decent meal!"

"Miss Hayes will understand," her mother said. "They'll blow the no-school signal at twelve, and she won't even plan to come. You'll see."

But as they hurried out, Annie glanced miserably at the apple pie just begun, the lobster kettle empty on the stove. On the busy dock, Annie forgot her problem. Most of the lobstermen were making their boats and gear secure against the winds and tides that were to come. Those who were just starting out to haul offered Annie and her mother their help. She thanked them, but politely refused.

"They have planned their time, too," she said as she guided the *Mary T.* beyond the breakwater.

The little lobster boat easily took the long swells. The staccato beat of the engine shattered the heavy stillness around them. Through her braced feet, Annie felt the throbbing power of her father's boat. Happy summer hours when she had helped with the hauling flowed behind her like the backwash of the *Mary T.* But now she was not along for the ride with her father in charge. She and her mother were on their own. And the short time they had was precious.

She narrowed her eyes against the steely sun and spotted the first familiar buoy, striped red and black with her father's colors. Her mother cut the motor as Annie leaned out with the hook to grasp the buoy line. Careful. No time for a second try. She snared the line and looped it around the winch, guiding the heavy pot up over the gunwale of the boat. As the *Mary T.* moved on, she seized the lobsters behind their waving claws and threw them, dripping, into the basket.

Again and again, Annie went through the same nightmarish motions until her legs ached from standing and her shoulders were stiff with weariness. But her heart swelled with pride. They were saving most of her father's catch, and—more important—most of his gear. Regretfully she eyed the deep-water pots as they passed them by. But time was running out. They would have to take their chances with the storm. Between stops, Annie stored the gear safely in the cabin. There would not be time to transfer the lobster pots from the cockpit once they got back.

It was nearly impossible to stand in the pitching boat. Annie gripped the winch. The rain came slowly at first, then with driving force.

"We're going in," called her mother.

The waves were mountainous now, even inside the breakwater, and the tide reached high up the beach. They ran alongside the pier and, without pegging the lobsters, dumped them into the "car" or lobster cage, built into their float. Wearily they anchored the *Mary T.* fore and aft in deep water. As they rowed into the cove, the wind began to whip the harbor like an eggbeater.

"Dad will be proud," her mother panted as they pulled the tender high onto the beach. She looked at Annie. "Don't worry about Miss Hayes. We'll ask her to come over next week."

They were halfway up the path when the wind struck, screaming as it lashed them with stinging sand. Heads bowed, they ran to the house. The wind slammed the door behind them.

The figure by the stove, clad in Mother's apron, hurried to help them out of their wet oilskins.

"Welcome home," said Miss Hayes with a wink at Annie. "Supper's almost ready."

A glance at her mother's tired face showed Annie that her mother's pleasure was as great as her own. While the two women exchanged news, Annie washed up for dinner and then stoked the fire in the hearth.

Outside, the storm struck with such fury that houses shook. But the boats in the harbor rode sturdily at anchor, and inside Annie's house everything was cozy and safe.

Over supper, Annie told the story of how they had hurried to pull the traps and save the gear before the storm struck.

"You're real islanders," her teacher smiled, and somehow it was a perfect compliment. "It was a fine thing for you both to do."

Then Miss Hayes explained how she had come early, hoping she could be of help during the storm.

"After all," she said, "I'm an islander now, too."

Annie held out her plate for another helping of Miss Hayes's apple pie. "I'll say you are!" she said.